THE

DREAMWORKS

BOSS BABY

FAMILY BUSINESS

JUNIOR NOVELIZATION

Adapted by Stacia Deutsch

Simon Spotlight

New York   London   Toronto   Sydney   New Delhi

SIMON SPOTLIGHT
An imprint of Simon & Schuster Children's Publishing Division
1230 Avenue of the Americas, New York, New York 10020
This Simon Spotlight edition August 2021
DreamWorks The Boss Baby: Family Business © 2021 DreamWorks Animation LLC. All Rights Reserved. All rights reserved, including the right of reproduction in whole or in part in any form. SIMON SPOTLIGHT and colophon are registered trademarks of Simon & Schuster, Inc. For information about special discounts for bulk purchases, please contact Simon & Schuster Special Sales at 1-866-506-1949 or business@simonandschuster.com.
Designed by Nicholas Sciacca
The text of this book was set in Bodoni.
Manufactured in the United States of America 0721 OFF
10 9 8 7 6 5 4 3 2 1
ISBN 978-1-5344-9866-2 (pbk)
ISBN 978-1-5344-9867-9 (hc)
ISBN 978-1-5344-9868-6 (eBook)

PROLOGUE

Tim Templeton was seven years old when his baby brother arrived. His parents were overjoyed and exhausted, but they didn't know the truth. Ted looked like a normal baby. But in the shadows and at night, he revealed his true identity. Ted Templeton was actually Boss Baby. Boss Baby had come to the Templeton's house from Baby Corp. on a top secret mission to save all babies, everywhere. He acted like a regular baby around adults, giggling and cooing and speaking gibberish. But the minute the grown-ups were out of sight (and earshot) he'd bark orders at Tim, like asking for his cell phone and a cappuccino. Tim became part of the mission. There were some ups and downs, but in the end, they were victorious. Babies were saved!

Boss Baby had the opportunity to return to Baby Corp. as the hero, but he chose to stay with his new family.

Now Tim was all grown up. He lived in the house he'd grown up in. He took care of his daughters, seven-year-old Tabitha and baby Tina, while his wife, Carol, worked.

Ted was grown up too. He was the boss of his own business.

Even their friends had grown up. Jimbo was the town mayor. He married Staci and they had a baby Tina's age. The triplets were police officers who patrolled on motorcycles.

Tim's life was good. His days were full of running errands, preparing meals, and helping with homework, but there was one thing missing: Ted. When they grew up, they grew apart. Tim and Ted didn't talk much anymore.

Little did they know, an exciting new Boss Baby adventure was just around the corner.

CHAPTER ONE

Tim had an incredible imagination. He closed his eyes, and suddenly it was as if his family was at the beach. It was a beautiful day, but then—a volcano erupted. It was exciting. It was terrifying. Hot lava spewed everywhere. Tim leaped into action, quickly rescuing Carol and Tina by moving them to safety. Then he went back to save Tabitha.

"Stay calm!" he told his daughter.

Tim was an expert in imaginary volcanos.

He turned his beach chair into a surfboard and rode the lava toward his daughter. Tim dodged and ducked and faced the danger with courage. Finally, the lava parted, allowing Tim's surfboard to pass safely through. Tim ground to a halt in front of his very focused, no-nonsense daughter, Tabitha. The daydream ended.

"Dad, what are you doing?!" Tabitha didn't have time for her dad's wild imagination today.

The volcano was a school science experiment with Mentos candy and soda. When mixed together, the Mentos would fizz into a massive foam.

Tabitha looked at the mess from the project. She knew she had to clean that up.

Tim still wanted to stay in the imaginary world. "Come on, this is the candy volcano of doom! You used to love it!" Clean up could wait. He wanted to get back to their pretend adventure.

Tabitha shook her head. "I'm trying to do my homework or *I'm* doomed." She gathered her stack of books and left the room.

"Oh . . . okay . . ." Tim watched Tabitha walk away. He sighed. "If there's one thing I've learned, it's that you're only a kid once. Once you grow up, you can never go back."

CHAPTER TWO

Tabitha was getting ready for bed. She smiled at her latest academic award, knowing there'd be more of those in her future. After checking out her poster of Rosie the Riveter and flexing a muscle, she set out her school uniform. The school's signature acorn button needed polishing, so she gave it a rub.

"Good night, Dr. Hawking!" Tabitha said to her goldfish.

Her bedtime reading was a book of math jokes. "Carry the four!" she said out loud, giggling. She was so into the book, she didn't notice her entire family had entered the room.

Tim said, "Hey there, Tabitha, it's the Good Night Show, live from your bedroom, starring Dad and Mom—"

Her mother added, "And special guest, baby Tina!"

Tabitha gave Tina a big kiss. "Good night, little Tina!"

Carol kissed Tabitha then held the baby tight. "Good night, sweetie."

"Good night, Mom!" Tabitha called out as Carol took Tina to her own room.

Tim sat on the edge of Tabitha's bed with his guitar. "Hey, what would you say to me helping you rehearse for the holiday pageant?" Tim asked. Snow was drifting by the window. "I can come to school with you, and we can get all your friends together, and we can rehearse together, and then go get some ice cream afterward, my treat."

Tabitha was horrified. "No! You can't do that. School rules. Um, liability issues. It's this whole thing. . . ." She was in a new school, the best school in town. Tim had never been there because her mom dropped her off on her way to work.

"Oh, right, right. Right. Oh! How about your favorite bedtime story?" Tim asked.

Tabitha shook her head. She summarized,

"Plenty of love to go around. Uncle Ted was a magical talking baby, there was a rocket full of puppies, and you saved the world."

"It was a good story, wasn't it?" He let the memory wash over him.

"Well, it didn't really make a lot of sense." Tabitha yawned. "Dad, I need to get some sleep. My schedule is brutal tomorrow."

"Yeah, my schedule's pretty brutal too," Tim told her with a sigh.

"Good night, Lam-Lam!" Tabitha kissed her favorite toy. Tim then placed it back on the shelf, next to a photo of Ted. She blew a kiss to the picture. "Good night, Uncle Ted. I hope to grow up and be a success just like you."

"Good night, Tabitha." Tim leaned in for a kiss, but Tabitha stuck out her hand for a shake. "Don't you think I'm a little old for that now?"

"Oh . . ." Tim was a little hurt, but he shook his daughter's hand.

"I think it's time we both grow up. I look forward to greeting you at the breakfast table!" Tabitha slid a sleep mask over her eyes and hugged her math joke book.

"Sweet dreams." Tim felt sad as he turned out her lights. He sighed. His little girl was growing up so fast.

After everyone was asleep, Tim went up into the attic.

All his favorite childhood things were there, making the attic look like it was the same room he slept in as a boy. He pulled out a box of Christmas ornaments and several colorful beads clattered to the floor.

Tim picked one up and flopped back onto his old bed.

"Where has the time gone?" Tim moaned.

"How should I know?!" A one-armed cloaked figure climbed slowly out of a storage box. "At long last! The sweet breath of freedom!"

Tim recognized his old, dear alarm clock. "Wizzie?!"

The clock, now with just one working arm, smacked Tim hard on the face. "You cast me into eternal darkness and wreaked havoc on my circadian rhythms!" Wizzie shook his arm angrily. The numbers on his clock spun.

"I'm sorry, Wizzie. Hey, but you look great though," Tim said.

"Except for the arm, you mean," Wizzie frowned. "You would never treat Lam-Lam this way."

"Well, I gave her to my daughter, Tabitha," Tim said.

"You have produced an heir, Timothy!" The wizard was proud to hear it.

"Two, actually!" Tim told him. He told the wizard that Tabitha was growing up too fast and he was worried about her. As he shared his concerns, Tim heard a strange noise coming through the attic floorboards. It sounded like it was coming from the baby's room.

Tim snuck downstairs. He pressed his ear to the door of Tina's nursery. He heard voices. Cautiously, Tim reached for the doorknob.

CHAPTER THREE

The baby was asleep. She looked like a little lump tucked safely under her blanket. In the crib, there was a toy phone. Tim held it up to his ear and said, "Hello?"

"If you'd like to make a call, please hang up and dial again." That was strange. But then Tim saw his own cell phone laying on the floor. He laughed. The voice must have been from his phone, not the toy.

He turned back to the crib to rearrange Tina's covers, only to discovered the lump was actually Story Time Bear. Where was Tina? A shadow passed behind him. He quickly turned to find a pair of eyes staring at him in the dark.

"Hi, Daddy." Tina laughed as Tim began to realize with shock his baby wasn't a regular baby. Baby Tina ripped off her pajamas to reveal a business suit underneath. "Yep! I'm in the family business!" She ran a hand over her suit. "It's a clip-on tie. You see, Baby Corp. is more of what I call a side—"

Tim missed the rest. He fainted.

Baby Tina smacked Tim's face until his eyes opened. "Daddy, how many fingers am I holding up?"

"Thursday?" Tim was confused.

"I should've given you a warning. I forgot you were an old man!" She gave Tim a sip of milk.

He spit it out. "Wait, wait. You're from Baby Corp.?"

"Baby Corp. is more of what I call a side hustle. The point is, I am all in on the Templetons. Go, Templetons! You guys *really* know how to baby a baby. I mean it's incredible! Not that it's all five stars, I have to say. You've got a lot of issues. We'll talk about that later." Once Tina started talking, it turned out she was very chatty.

Tim's shock turned to excitement. "Oh my gosh, I can't believe this! Hey, wanna go scare Mom? Or Tabitha?"

Tina insisted Tim listen to her. "There's a crisis at Baby Corp.!"

"What is it this time? Kittens?!" Tim asked.

Tina was serious. "This time it's even worse!"

"Worse than kittens?!" Tim wasn't a fan of kittens.

"Yes! That's why I volunteered for this super-secret assignment," Tina said.

The same feelings he'd had as a child came rushing back. "I want to help! What do you want me to do?"

"That's the spirit! You're exactly who I need!" Tina was thrilled.

"Yes!" This was great. What was his mission?

"Get Uncle Ted," Tina said. Tim frowned. "What's with the face? Baby Corp. can't wait any longer. All the pressure is on me. When I volunteered for this gig I thought it would be easy, but you two *never* see each other. It's so sad."

"Sad? Yeah, maybe, a little. I don't know." Tim realized how far apart he and his brother had grown. They hadn't talked in a long while.

"You have to get him here for the holidays." Tina had a plan. She handed her father his cell phone.

"No, I'm not gonna call him right now." He took it, but wouldn't dial.

Tina pressed him to explain why he refused to call his own brother.

"There's no point, okay? I call him. I invite him. He never shows up. He's always got a work meeting or a business trip or a conference call. All he cares about is work. After a while, you just stop trying." Tim shrugged. "I guess sometimes you grow up, and grow apart."

Baby Tina thought about it a minute then said, "Daddy, don't say no. What if everybody said no? Nothing would happen, nothing would get off the ground! You gotta wake up every day and you gotta say yes! Yes! Yes!" She held up his phone. "Surprise me, say yes!"

Tim scooped up Tina and set her back into her crib next to her Story Time Bear. He put a stuffed horse in the crib too. "It's late," Tim told her. "We can work on this tomorrow, okay?"

Tina tossed the horse at him.

Tim scooped it up. "Oh, whoopsie, your little

horsey fell off." He put it back in the crib and headed to the door. "Another day won't hurt, right? Good night, sweetie."

As soon as the door shut, Tina sat up and pressed a rewind button on the chest of Story Time Bear. She'd recorded the conversation.

"Good night, sweetie." She rewound more. "Fell off. Horsey." More rewinding. Near the beginning, she stopped. "Tabitha?!"

Tina grinned. She had all the words she needed.

CHAPTER FOUR

The next morning, Tim was brushing his teeth when the whole house began to shake.

Tabitha looked up from her homework. Baby Tina's eyes lit up. Tim looked out the window. A helicopter was landing in the street in front of the house. A mysterious bundled-up figure exited the helicopter and strode to the front door.

When Tim cracked the door open, Ted pushed past him to come inside. "Where is she?!" He looked frantically around for Tabitha.

She came into the hallway, excited to see her uncle. Ted immediately knelt down to examine her. "Which arm is it? Left or right?" He looked for bruises. "Is it your fibula?" He checked her legs. "Talk to me." He wasn't finding an obvious injury. He checked her eyes, "Good dilation." Then said, "Open up, say, 'Ahhhh.'"

She was clearly fine. Ted didn't understand.

He'd come as soon as he'd gotten the message that she'd fallen off the pony he'd bought her as a gift. Her name was Precious, and she lived in the backyard, and she didn't like Tim.

"Tim left me a voice mail," Ted explained. He held up his phone and played the garbled message.

"Hello. This is your brother," Tim was saying. *"Help? Tabitha fell off horsey. Good night, sweetie."* It was clear, but oddly choppy.

"I swear I didn't leave that message!" Tim realized who did it. He glanced at Tina who was looking as innocent as possible. Tim couldn't reveal that she wasn't really a baby, so he said, "I butt-dialed! While I was talking in my sleep, I do that sometimes."

Ted eyed his brother. "You sleep-butt-dialed me?"

Tim was desperate for this to end. "Yep. With my butt."

"I knew there must be a perfectly *logical* explanation." Ted stared at his brother. Tim stared back.

Everyone was so happy Ted was there that Tim wasn't surprised when they asked him to stay for Christmas. Ted, of course, was too busy.

Tim decided to tell Ted about Tina and Baby Corp. They went into the kitchen. Tim took Tina along and set her in her high chair, then he whispered to Ted while peeking at Tina.

"She's been sent from up there," Tim revealed, pointing to the ceiling.

"Upstairs?" Ted asked.

Tim remembered, but Ted had forgotten the past. "Baby Corp.! A secret corporation run by babies!"

Ted gave Tim a concerned look. "Tim, I'm going to give you the name of a doctor, Roy Federman. Just tell him I sent you, okay?"

In the other room, Tabitha pressed her ear against a cup. She held the cup to the door. She struggled to hear and was having trouble making out the exact words. When Ted and Tim began to fight, her mom decided that they should let the adults work it out. She took Tabitha to get a Christmas tree.

"But we already have a Christmas tree," Tabitha protested as Carol tossed her a coat. Carol led Tabitha out of the house and toward the car.

Tim was determined to make his brother remember. He told Ted that Tina could talk. That didn't work. Ted just thought Tim was using his vivid imagination again. Tim needed to prove it.

He held up a pacifier. "Suck it, Ted."

Ted was offended. "I beg your pardon?"

"You, suck," Tim said.

"No, no, Tim. You suck," Ted countered. Their argument got louder and louder.

To end it, baby Tina opened her briefcase and cleared her throat. "Excuse me, I hate to interrupt, I mean, it was a riveting conversation. But may I make a suggestion?" She stuffed pacifiers into both their mouths. "Why don't you both suck it?"

Ted mumbled, "She can talk?!"

Tim sucked his pacifier. "A lot!"

In one swift move, she tore off her onesie. Underneath was her suit. Tina popped a pacifier into her own mouth while saying, "Buckle up, boys!"

CHAPTER FIVE

Tim and Ted spiraled through space and time, screaming, until they landed safely at Baby Corp. Headquarters.

Ted's memory came back. He looked around and said, "I'm home." They were standing in front of a huge statue of Boss Baby.

"I did single-handedly save the company." Ted grinned.

"Double-handedly, right? We were partners." Tim looked around the plaza. There was no statue of him.

Tim frowned all the way to the elevator. And all the way up to the top floor with its big windows and computer stations. Here, some babies worked on projects while other babies were sent down to families. There were files on all the babies.

Then Tina told her uncle that she'd seen his file. Ted wanted to know what it said, but she wouldn't tell him. The conversation about files ended when they reached the control center of Baby Corp. In the middle of the room was a huge globe. Babies used long sticks to push toy models around the world.

Baby Tina gave the tour. "This is the crisis center. This is where we monitor all threats to babies around the world."

Ted surveyed the screens. "What's the crisis?"

Baby Tina pointed to the screens as a prerecorded film began to roll.

"Just imagine baby surgeons, uh-oh! Or baby astronauts. Floaty, floaty, float!" A man who looked like he was a college professor, smoking a pipe and wearing a tweed jacket, stepped fully into view. *"Yes, babies are going to run the world one day. And that day is coming sooner than you think."* He introduced himself. *"Hello, my name is Dr. Erwin Armstrong, founder of the Acorn Center for Advanced Childhood."*

"That's Tabitha's school!" Tim had goose bumps. What was going on?!

Dr. Armstrong surrounded them, his face on every screen. He was standing in a classroom between two students. *"Here at the center, we believe babies are the ultimate learning machines. Isn't that right, little Nathan?"*

"Yeah! Okay!" Nathan agreed. Next to him, a girl named Meghan, nodded.

Dr. Armstrong disappeared for a second, then materialized in front of a giant clock.

"The only thing holding your child back is you." He stared out from the screen. *"You!"*

Tim pointed to himself and wondered if he was really holding Tabitha back from learning. "This explains why Tabitha's been pulling away from me. It's the school!" he realized.

Dr. Armstrong turned to the class of students behind him. *"Everybody wave! Bye, Mommy. Bye, Daddy!"*

"Bye, Mommy. Bye, Daddy!" the kids repeated in unison. Then the video went dark.

Baby Tina explained, "In the past six months, these schools have been popping up all over the world. If Armstrong's philosophy keeps spreading, it could be the end of childhood."

Ted didn't mind. "Childhood was the worst three years of my life."

"That's so sad," Tina told him. "You probably just didn't do it right." Her face brightened. "But luckily, you get a second chance!"

She hurried them through the busy, crowded floor and into a stark white room where baby scientists in white hazmat suits and welding masks were mixing a glowing baby formula. Tina explained, "Baby Corp. has developed a new superduper baby formula that can turn a grown-up back into a baby."

Ted stared at the formula. "You want me to be a baby?!"

"Hey, it's what you do best!" Tim poked him in the arm and laughed.

Tina told her uncle, "You can infiltrate the school and find out what Dr. Armstrong is really up to. Baby Corp. will take care of the rest!"

CHAPTER SIX

Back in the Templeton kitchen, baby Tina opened her briefcase and very carefully set a bottle of the powerful formula on the counter.

"It's the perfect disguise!" Tina said. "And it only lasts forty-eight teensy-weensy hours."

Ted nervously read the baby bottle formula label. "Warning: may cause drooling, babbling, emotional outbursts, fits of laughter, loss of bowel control, and chubby thighs?" He squirted a drop of the formula onto his finger and suddenly, his entire hand shrunk!

"Ah! My texting hand!" Ted tried to shake it off, but the hand just got smaller. While Ted was trying to figure out how he'd ever text again, Tim grabbed the formula bottle and took a big gulp. He wasn't going to be left out of the mission. It was his daughter's school after all. A moment later, he was a teenager.

Once Tim drank it, Ted became even more competitive. "It's mine!" He wrestled the bottle from Tim. He also took a big gulp. Now, Ted was a teenager too. "I'm better at this kind of thing!" he declared.

The brothers tackled each other, fighting for the bottle and control of Baby Corp.'s mission. Ted had it and took a sip. Tim chased Ted. When he caught him, he knocked the bottle out of Ted's hand and took a long gulp. Ted and Tim continued to shrink. Their clothing was getting bigger and bigger.

"Hey!" Tim hit the wall and lost a few more years.

"You always have to be the hero, don't you?" Young Tim accused Young Ted.

"What's that supposed to mean?" Ted angrily sprayed Tim's legs with the formula. Tim's legs shrunk, but he kept chasing after Ted.

Tim was grumpy, muttering, "We never see him"—(meaning Ted)—"and all of a sudden he shows up with a pony—"

"You're just jealous, helmet head!" Ted declared. They rolled across the carpet.

"She's my daughter!" Tim stomped on Ted's coat. Ted fell back into him.

"She's my niece!" Ted said, declaring he'd be the one to protect her.

"Mommy says no running in the house!" Tina shouted after them.

Ted took one last gulp, then Tim shoved him so hard that Ted fell out of his clothing. Underneath was his suit. Uncle Ted was now Boss Baby.

"It's not personal. It's business, *Leslie*," Ted said, calling Tim by his middle name.

"Well I put my family first, *Lindsey*." That was Ted's middle name.

Tina finally had enough. She stepped up to her dad and uncle who were locked together and rolling across the floor. "Okay, time out! This has gone far enough!"

Carol and Tabitha were back.

"Hey, we're home, and we got another tree!"

Tabitha announced, her voice echoing through the house.

Tim and Boss Baby looked at each other. Tim was back to being seven years old. Ted was Boss Baby again. This was bad. When Tabitha and Carol left, they'd been adults. They hurried as fast as they possibly could in their new littler bodies, up the stairs with Tina.

Tim could hear Tabitha and Carol struggling to bring the new Christmas tree into the living room.

"Where are you guys?" Carol called up the steps.

"Tell her you're packing!" Tina suggested to Tim.

Tim tried that. "We're upstairs, packing!"

"Packing? For what?" Carol called up again.

Tim and Ted couldn't just disappear from the house when they left for the Baby Corp. mission. They needed a good cover story. Tim shouted down the stairs. "We're going on a brother bonding trip!"

"Now?! But your parents are coming tomorrow!"

Carol was clearly concerned. She started climbing the stairs. Tim and Boss Baby could hear the footsteps getting closer.

What were they going to do? They had to make it seem like they'd left the house.

Carol couldn't see them like this. . . .

CHAPTER SEVEN

As Carol continued up the stairs, Tina caused a distraction. She slid down the stair railing like a roller coaster. It was reckless, and so much fun! She trusted her mom to stop and catch her before she crashed!

"Tina! What are you doing?!" Carol gasped and put Tina in her playpen, while Tabitha struggled to arrange the new tree next to the old one.

"Hello? A little help here!" Tabitha called. The tree was tipping over.

"Sorry, Tabitha. Hold it up!" Carol jumped in to help.

While her mom and Tabitha were busy, Tina snuck Ted's cellphone from her onesie and made a call to his helicopter pilot. "This is Ted Templeton, a man." She tried to make her voice low and gravelly. "You can go ahead and take off. I have urgent family business." The pilot seemed surprised at that news, so she felt the need to say, "Yes, I have a family."

"Time for us to go!" Tim slid by the living room, staying out of view. He also was talking in a low, adult voice.

"Now?!" Carol was busy with the tree, so she didn't see Ted and Tim bolt toward the front door.

Boss Baby was right behind him. "Yeah. My helicopter's double-parked!"

Tim called, "Bye!" He slammed the front door, but they didn't really leave.

While Tabitha and Carol watched the helicopter leave, Tim and Boss Baby ran straight to Tina's room and hid there.

Later that night, after her mom had put her to bed, Tina sat up. Tim and Boss Baby were under the crib. They crawled out, and Tina began the meeting. "I've decided who's going on the mission." She gave them her baby clothes to put on, then announced, "Both of you."

"No!" Boss Baby was furious. "I work alone. Or, at least, not with him." Boss Baby pointed at Tim.

"Hey! There's no *I* in team," Tim said, trying to convince Boss Baby.

"Actually, there's no *U* in team either, but there is an *M-E*." Boss Baby wanted to go alone.

Tina was in charge, so when she said they were both going, that was the final decision. She opened a dresser drawer, revealing a hidden cache of spy-baby gadgets.

"We have secret intel that Armstrong leaves his office every morning at eleven fifteen. You need to sneak in there and plant these surveillance devices and report back to me." She handed Tim a microphone disguised as a flower. Boss Baby took a listening device that looked like a ladybug.

"Man, so cool!" Tim gushed, holding the flower right in front of his eye.

Boss Baby jumped into checking his device out. "Right. Testing."

Tina logged into her tablet, where she could see the closeup of Tim's eyeball and the sound waves from Boss Baby talking.

She gave the final instructions. "Now, I've arranged for a school bus to be here at eight a.m. sharp. Do not be late!"

On their way to his attic "room," Tim overheard a conversation between Tabitha and Carol.

"Oh, sweetie, don't worry. I'm sure your dad'll be back in time to see you in the pageant," Carol said. Then Tabitha said something Tim couldn't hear. But he heard Carol's response.

"What? Don't you want him to come?" Carol asked. Tim held his breath to hear the answer.

"I guess." It wasn't very enthusiastic.

"Of course, you do." Carol didn't press with more questions. "Now go back to sleep." The light flicked off.

Tim settled Boss Baby into an open dresser drawer for the night. He lay on his old bed. It was an exhausting day, but he couldn't sleep. For a long time, he stared at the ceiling. When he finally closed his eyes, he could hear the conversation between Carol and Tabitha playing over and over in his head.

Then, suddenly, Tim started to fall. What was happening? He was sinking though his mattress, into a dark void. All thoughts of home and Tabitha and the mission faded as Tim began to scream.

CHAPTER EIGHT

It was a nightmare.

Tim was an adult again, and he was on a witness stand. The courtroom was crowded.

Boss Baby was the judge. He banged a gavel. "The trial of Timothy Leslie Templeton is now in session!"

"Trial?!" Tim had no idea what this was about. "Wait, what are the charges?"

"Fraud." Boss Baby gave him a hard stare. "Claiming to be the World's Best Dad."

The nightmare made Tim sweat. He tried to protest. "But I never said—"

Boss Baby slammed down Tim's World's Best Dad mug and shouted, "Exhibit A!"

"Oh, come on, that was a gift!" Tim countered. He discovered that his attorney was Precious, the pony Ted gave Tabitha and who didn't like him. His parents "testified" against him. Wizzie said Tim had been the one to break his arm, even though everyone knew it had been Ted. This trial was out of control and Tim didn't know what to do.

Judge Boss Baby read the jury's decision. "We the jury find the defendant . . ."

His own family shouted, "A failure!"

Tim turned to Tabitha, who was there, but hadn't spoken. She was reading at a table next to him. "Tabitha, please help me out?" he begged.

"Dad, the homework! It's just too much!" Tabitha began spinning, and then she was sucked into her books.

"Tabitha!" Tim cried.

Wizzie pulled a lever. "Time's up!" *WHOOSH*! A trapdoor opened beneath Tim, and he dropped straight into a giant World's Worst Dad mug.

Tim woke up.

In the morning, Tim was groggy when he glanced over at the clock and noticed the time. He jumped out of bed, shouting, "We overslept!" Tim opened the window. He saw that Carol was pulling out of the driveway, driving Tabitha to school. That was bad, but worse, the bus that he and Boss Baby were meant to be on was already coming down the street.

Tim rushed over to the drawer Boss Baby was sleeping in. "Get up. We gotta go! C'mon, we're gonna be late."

"I'll email it to you!" Boss Baby yawned, shaking off his own, successful business dream. "What's going on?"

Tim grabbed the ladybug microphone and the flower camera and shoved them into a backpack. "We gotta go!" Tim and Boss Baby skateboarded down the attic ladder. They were half dressed in Tina's clothes. The laundry chute was a shortcut downstairs, but it was too high for Boss Baby to climb in.

"Upsies! I need upsies!" he called to Tim. Tim pulled him into the chute after him, and they tumbled down into the wash basket. They needed clothing that fit and the only thing Tim could find was their old matching sailor outfits. There was no time to look for other clothing. Tim raced out the door to catch the bus, with Boss Baby behind him. It was too late. The bus disappeared around a corner.

Boss Baby took matters in his own hands. He whistled, and Precious appeared from behind the house.

"Precious, my noble steed." Boss Baby fed Precious a carrot. "We must not be late for our first day of school."

"This pony doesn't like me," Tim groaned as he got on. There was no other choice. Boss Baby rode like a professional, while Tim could barely hang on.

"Tallyho, Precious!" Boss Baby leaned in and Precious gracefully jumped in and out of several backyards.

"It's not that she doesn't like you, Tim," Boss Baby said. "She just doesn't respect you." The horse ran past a snowman. The head got stuck on Tim as they wove through street traffic.

"Go left! Go left!" Tim directed them toward the school.

They raced through a building, then burst

through the top window, out onto the roof of the coffee shop next door. The giant coffee cup from the coffee shop's sign got stuck behind the pony, and Precious pulled it like a sled.

Just as Tim tumbled backward into the giant coffee cup, his phone rang. "Oh no, it's Carol!"

Boss Baby tried to stop him from answering, but Tim picked up anyway.

"Tim! How's your bonding trip?" Carol asked.

The sleigh coffee cup hit a bump, and Tim flew into the air. For a second, he glanced over at the car next to them. It was Carol! And Tabitha! With baby Tina in the back.

Baby Tina saw her dad and muttered, "Oh no . . ."

"We're, uh . . ." Tim started when Boss Baby grabbed his phone.

In a deep voice, Boss Baby assured Carol. "We're . . . uh, rebooting our relationship and restoring the closeness that we once felt." The cup-sled caught air, landed on a frozen river, and skidded through a hockey game.

The noise made Carol ask, "Where are you?"

Boss Baby quickly handed the phone back to Tim.

"Uh . . . a hockey game!" Tim said, which was totally true.

The horse and cup zoomed back onto the main road. They sped past a trio of policemen. It was the triplets Boss Baby knew when he was first sent to the Templetons!

"Busted," all three chanted as they flicked on the sirens.

Carol heard the sirens over the phone. "Is that the police?"

This was bad. Tim pretended he didn't hear the sirens, but the noise was so loud, he barely heard Carol say, "I want to remind you that Tabitha's pageant is tomorrow night."

Oh no! Tim looked like a child. He was on a mission with his brother, who looked like Boss Baby. Still, he promised, "I will be there! In one shape or another!"

It was hard for Tim to concentrate on the call as Precious dragged them through town. They stormed past Mayor Jimbo, who stood in front of a massive

Christmas tree covered in lights. It was beautiful, right up until Precious leaped through the tree. The horse got tangled in lights, forcing the tree over, and dragging it away. Ornaments scraped the sidewalk. The tree burst into flames!

It was so chaotic that Tim almost forgot that Carol was still on the phone "Tim?"

"Uh, Carol? You're breaking up. I'm losing you!" Tim sputtered, looking at the horse in front of him and the flaming tree dragging behind. "See you at the pageant!" Tim said. "Gotta go, bye!"

Tim hung up moments before the massive Christmas tree began rolling, turning into a giant snowball. Everything in its path was sucked into the ball. Decorations, the triplets, and even Jimbo, all disappeared. Tim, Boss Baby, and Precious were sucked under the snowball as well, but they popped out and managed to stay on top as the ball kept growing.

The snowball was now next to Carol's car. Tina watched from her car seat, horrified that they were going to get sucked into it too. In a swift move, she used a shark grabber toy to reach the car's emergency brake, and yanked it back with all her strength. The car skidded to a stop in front of the school. Precious, Boss Baby, and Tim also jumped free. The snowball rolled safely by.

To Tim's great shock, they'd made it to school on time. And yet, behind them, nearly the entire town was in complete shambles.

CHAPTER NINE

Boss Baby surveyed the damage. It was a lot. Not good. "Huh. I'll send them a check." At least it would all get fixed nicely.

The school sign read: THE ACORN CENTER FOR ADVANCED CHILDHOOD.

It was a brand-new, sleek, modern building. Tim thought it looked a like a stack of books mixed with a prison. "Whoa. This place looks evil," Tim remarked. He looked at their sailor outfits. They were going to need uniforms if they were going to get inside.

Boss Baby had that problem covered. He threw money along the sidewalk as they headed toward the school. He waited until some children began to pick up the cash, then continued to leave a trail that led behind some bushes. When the kids were out of view, Tim and Boss Baby followed them. When Tim and Boss Baby came back out from the bushes, *they* were wearing school uniforms. The kids were wearing old sailor suits and clutching wads of cash.

Every student had an acorn button on their uniform. When they reached the main doorway, the buttons turned yellow, blue, red, or green. There were paths to follow according to their acorn.

At the school entrance, Tim handed Boss Baby the ladybug-microphone and said, "We gotta split up."

Tim saw Tabitha nearby. She was getting out of the car. Her acorn glowed blue.

Tim watched Tina blow on the back window to steam it up. She wrote TEEMWORK! on the glass as Carol pulled away.

Boss Baby watched the car pull out and said, "Apparently there's no *A* in teamwork either."

Tim wanted to follow Tabitha, but Boss Baby held him back. "Not so fast. I'm blue. You're yellow," Boss Baby said. He pointed at a miniature yellow train loaded with babies. "You're over there, in the choo choo."

Tim didn't want to be yellow. He wanted to stay with Tabitha. While Boss Baby was telling Tim they had to meet at eleven fifteen at Dr. Armstrong's office, Tim straightened Boss Baby's necktie. And switched their acorns.

Tim put Boss Baby in the yellow train with the babies. "I'm not yellow, I'm blue!" Boss Baby realized he'd been tricked. As the train disappeared into the school, Tim could hear Boss Baby shouting, "I'm blue! I'm blue!"

Tim followed the blue line. He went through broad doors into a giant atrium. A huge tree grew in the middle. An acorn-shaped tree house was high in the top branches.

Dr. Armstrong was in the atrium, greeting the kids as they carefully followed the colored lines to their classrooms. "Welcome, children! Thank you for choosing to be excellent."

The yellow tram passed by overhead. Tim could hear Boss Baby still ranting, "I'm blue! I'm blue!"

Tim smiled to himself as he dutifully followed the blue line to an open door. When he entered,

Tabitha was already in the front row reading. This was his chance to "make friends" with her.

"Hello," he said.

"Hello," she replied. "Nice plant." Tim was carrying the flower-camera.

"Oh yes." He sputtered an excuse. "This is my emotional support plant. Hi. I'm new here."

Tim tried to find a seat near Tabitha, but Nathan, the kid from the video, blocked him.

"Can't sit here. Or here. Or there," Nathan told Tim, pointing at empty desks. "Seating position is determined by class rank. We can't possibly include your data given that the rigor of your previous school is an unknown variable,"

"Sick burn, Nathan!" Meghan, from the video, said.

Tabitha offered him her desk. Tim was so pleased with the way she was helping out a new kid. And even though he *was* that new kid, he still felt fatherly.

A robotic cart with a monitor for a head rolled up to the front of the class. It booted up. Tim stared at the monitor as the computerized version of Dr. Armstrong appeared. "Hey, I'm excited! As you can see, we have a new colleague joining us today."

"Hello," Tim cautiously greeted him.

"New colleague, why don't you introduce yourself?"

"My name is T—" Whoa. That was close. "Uh, Marcos . . . Marcos Lightspeed."

Lights on the bottom of Tim's desk spun around until the letters rearranged themselves into MARCOS LIGHTSPEED.

"Marcos Lightspeed!" Dr. Armstrong said. "Colorful, characterful, and I like it. In any case, welcome, Marcos, to the blue room. Our most advanced class."

A flash came from Dr. Armstrong's monitor as Tim's photo was taken. Then, Tim noticed that a leaderboard was projected on the wall with each student's picture, above a graph line representing their progress. Tim's terrible picture appeared in a spot between photos of Tabitha and Nathan.

"This is rarified air we're breathing! Here at

the Acorn Center, we believe that all competition is . . ." He held up a finger, conducting the class.

"Healthy competition!" the children recited.

In the yellow room, there was chaos. A naked baby was running wild. Other babies were singing, biting, throwing toys, or wrestling. There was no teacher, just a locked door and some playful googly eyes on the wall that seemed to be watching them.

Boss Baby breathed heavily. "I'm having a panic attack. There must be a way out of here." One of the eyes focused on him. "I have to get out of here." Boss Baby searched for an exit.

A creepy-looking girl came up behind him. "Hi," she said. Then, "Don't look at me."

That worked fine. Boss Baby was eager not to look at her. "Okay." This room, and the noisy, wild kids in it, were more than he could handle. He had to escape.

CHAPTER TEN

"Our first subject today is particle physics!" Dr. Armstrong announced.

"Yes!" Nathan punched the air, while Tim slunk down in his desk, hoping never to be called on.

Dr. Armstrong asked, "Who knows which scientist first theorized that the universe has a limit beyond which the laws of physics break down?"

Tim kept his hands to his side, but every other kid, including Tabitha, raised their hand.

"Señor Lightspeed?" Or course, Dr. Armstrong called on Tim anyway.

Tim didn't know. A buzzer sounded and a giant red X lit up on the front of his desk.

"Okay, anybody else?" Dr. Armstrong asked the class.

"Right here!" Nathan had the answer, but Tabitha beat him to it.

"Max Planck!" She gave the right answer with a quick sideways glance at Nathan.

"That's correct!" Dr. Armstrong said. "Tabitha has set the bar, first one on the board! Way to go, Tabitha."

Her desk glowed with a green check and Tabitha's name moved up the classroom leaderboard while Nathan's name moved down a spot.

Nathan sneered, "You're going down, Templeton."

"Bring it on, Nathan," Tabitha challenged.

"Next subject." The entire classroom rotated until the students faced a new direction to start the new topic.

Dr. Armstrong announced, "Ancient Greece"

"Opa!" The class greeted the topic.

Tim was a beat behind them. He echoed, "Oprah!"

In the yellow room, Boss Baby climbed onto a desk to address the crowd. "Attention! Attention, everyone!" he said. "Who wants to go outside and play? Does that sound fun? Who's with me?"

The babies all cheered and clapped.

Boss Baby asked for ideas on how they could get outside.

A girl raised her hand. "Oh, oh! Me! Me!" She looked like Bo Peep from the nursery rhyme.

"You, Bo Peep." Boss Baby called on her.

"We can build a hot-air balloon out of Popsicle sticks and bubble gum," she said, grinning.

"And how would it fly?" Boss Baby asked.

She knew exactly. "Pixie dust!"

Boss Baby shook his head, looking to see if anyone else had a realistic idea, when he noticed a baby who was gluing crayons to his face. "I like glue," Glue Baby said while rolling across the floor. Construction paper and other materials stuck to him.

Boss Baby put his head down in his hand. What a nightmare! But then his eyes caught a ray of light coming through a high window. The window was open a crack, but that was a start!

Boss Baby eyed the surveillance cameras. He quickly distributed cans of soft clay to the babies and told them to make balls. Then he arranged the babies into an assembly line to make catapults using Popsicle sticks and blocks. When the catapults were ready, he directed them to load the clay balls onto the homemade catapults and commanded, "Fire!"

SPLAT! SPLAT! The clay covered the googly-eyed surveillance cameras.

"Yes!" Boss Baby cheered. Escape was so close he could taste it.

In the blue room, the students were working on their chemistry projects. Tabitha was far ahead of them all.

"I found a cure!" Tabitha raised a test tube.

"She did it!" Tim began to do a very dad-like victory dance, pumping his fists when he accidentally knocked into some surrounding beakers. They rolled off the table and exploded. More and more tubes exploded until finally, the room's built-in water sprinklers kicked on to put out the fires.

When it was quiet again, the board in Tim's room lit up with the names of students in order of their successes. Tabitha was number one. Nathan was last.

"No!" Nathan was mad. He felt he deserved a higher spot.

"You'll be singing a different tune at rehearsal—the wrong tune," Nathan warned Tabitha.

Meghan laughed, telling Nathan, "You're so funny! Hilarious!" To Tabitha, she said, "Yeah, Templeton, don't be late!"

"Late." Tim heard the word and realized, "I'm late!" It was almost eleven fifteen. He should have left to meet Boss Baby already.

"Next subject," Dr. Armstrong announced.

The room began to spin again.

CHAPTER ELEVEN

Tim needed to go to the principal's office. He could only think of one solid way to get there, and that meant he needed to be sent there for bad behavior. He went to the bathroom with a marker and gave himself tattoos and a mustache. He rolled up his sleeves and tried to look tough. Then he burst back into the classroom with his new, terrible attitude.

"What's up, y'all?" Tim faced the virtual Armstrong, waiting for his punishment.

"Listen, you know, I acknowledge your anger. It's very feisty. But please sit down." Dr. Armstrong was calm.

Tim didn't sit, instead he drew a mustache on Dr. Armstrong's screen. In an evil voice, he asked, "Are we gonna have a 'talk' in your 'office'?"

Instead of kicking Tim out of class, Dr. Armstrong sent him to a time-out room called the Box. The other students were scared for him. Tim tried to protest that he needed to go to the office instead, but Dr. Armstrong's TV monitor rolled up and shoved him forward.

The time-out room looked like a day spa. Walls made of screens displayed soothing ocean scenes. There were aromatherapy candles and soft music.

"Relax," Dr. Armstrong told Tim.

The one and only door closed, clicked, and locked.

Boss Baby attempted to get the yellow room babies to make a scaffold out of toys so he could reach the window. But it crashed. Coming out of the wreckage, he looked at his watch. He was late. His only escape plan was ruined.

Suddenly there was a voice.

"Glue is bad." Glue Baby was stuck to the wall and he crawled up it like Spider-Man.

Boss Baby saw the potential! "Glue is good!"

Boss Baby, his hands sticky with glue, crawled

up and through the window, leaving the room. Slowly moving across the ceiling to avoid detection, he headed toward the principal's office. He was close to Dr. Armstrong's office when the glue stopped working and Boss Baby fell, landing face-first on the carpet.

"Ptlzzpfth!" He spit out fibers. "Ugh! It's like they always say, if you want something done right, you have to do it without your brother." Boss Baby was going to place the bug inside all by himself. To his great surprise, when he entered the office, Dr. Armstrong was there to greet him.

"You are, if I may say so, extremely intelligent," Dr. Armstrong said, complimenting him. A chair automatically rolled up and scooped Boss Baby into the seat.

"Go on . . ." Boss Baby liked a compliment. He yanked one of his still-sticky hands off an armrest, but he only managed to get stuck more.

"You had no business being in the yellow room, did you?" Dr. Armstrong really understood Boss Baby.

"It was sabotage!" Boss Baby said.

"Sabotage, exactly. Jealousy. Fear. Hey, I've faced the same obstacles. In fact, you know, you remind me a lot of myself when I was your age." Dr. Armstrong's face softened as he said, "Which is now." In one swift move, he spit his dentures across the desk, gripped the lapel of his tweed jacket, and revealed the truth:

DR. ARMSTRONG WAS A BABY! He walked around in an adult-size robotic suit to fool everybody! But in reality, he wasn't any bigger than Boss Baby!

Boss Baby couldn't believe his eyes. He made sure the bug, and therefore Tina, could hear him by speaking super clearly and very loudly. "He's a— you're a baby! I repeat, you're a baby."

"So surprised you said it twice! Unfortunately, people are not ready for a baby in a position of power. Yet!" Dr. Armstrong peeled off his facial hair and placed it aside.

Boss Baby tried to discreetly place the bug, but it was stuck to his hands. When he shook it free, the bug flew across the room, landing in Dr. Armstrong's bowl of candy.

"You know, I could use somebody like you, with a superior intelligence like my own," Dr. Armstrong told Boss Baby.

"Really?" Boss Baby said, staring in horror as Dr. Armstrong reached into the candy bowl and ate the ladybug listening device.

He licked his lips. "Somebody who can truly comprehend what I'm trying to accomplish."

Boss Baby needed to know more.

"We have a secret level, for very special babies. The best of the best. The elite." Dr. Armstrong hit a button and Boss Baby's acorn turned from yellow to bright purple. "There's a meeting today after school." He handed Boss Baby a lollipop. "We may be small, but we're about to teach grown-ups a big lesson." Just then, a bell rang. Dr. Armstrong stood. "Ooo, time for recess! Bye-bye!"

The office opened and Boss Baby's chair flew backward, out of the office. It dumped him in the hall. The chair cushion was stuck to his bottom and the sucker was stuck to his face, but he'd been invited to Dr. Armstrong's inner circle.

CHAPTER TWELVE

Tina was at home watching a video of a toy bunny playing the piano. Carol walked past. The second Carol was gone, Tina swiped over to a feed from her dad and uncle. She rolled through the tape until she found the audio from Boss Baby's bug.

"You're a baby! I repeat, you're a baby!"

When Carol came back into the room, Tina switched back to bunny playing a piano. Carol walked away again and Tina flipped over to the camera Tim was assigned.

Tim was in the time out room, fast asleep.

"Oh, Daddy." She sighed.

"Your time out has concluded." The soothing voice in the time-out room woke Tim up.

Tim shook himself further awake and a few minutes later, stepped out into the bright sun of the playground, where a burly baby bodyguard tried to stop him from entering the yellow play area.

Boss Baby instructed the guard to let Tim approach. "You failed me. I was desperate. I crawled. I did things with glue that I'm not proud of," Boss Baby said. "But I made it all the way to Armstrong's office. And then—"

"I was in the Box, okay?!" Tim tried to explain.

"The Box?" Whispers went throughout the yellow play area.

Tim used their awe to make himself into a hero. "Yeah, that's right! Show a little respect!"

The yellow play area babies all scattered.

Boss Baby wasn't impressed. "See, Tim: this is why I work alone. I'll succeed in the mission. You can take the pony home."

"The only thing you're ever going to succeed at is being alone," Tim spat out before walking away.

Tim walked through the hallway. Everything was ruined and it was all his fault.

"You're blowing it, Templeton!" Nathan said, his voice booming through the hall. It took Tim a moment to realize Nathan wasn't talking to him.

"Yeah, Templeton!" Meghan echoed.

"I'm trying . . ." That was Tabitha's voice.

Tim hurried, following the voices to a nearby room. Tim peeked into a rehearsal room where the students were practicing for the big school pageant.

Nathan was directing, and choreographing, while Meghan played piano. It was obviously not the first time they'd been through the song. Tabitha looked like she might cry. The other children moaned as she messed up again.

"I just can't do it right now, okay!" Tabitha hit her limit. Head down in shame, she left the room.

Tim was heartbroken seeing Tabitha that way.

Nathan released the other kids. "All right, all right, all right! See you at the pageant tomorrow. Beat it!" When the room emptied, Tim heard Meghan begging, "I want to sing the song!"

"No, I want to see her fail," Nathan replied with a sinister laugh.

Tim made sure they hadn't seen him, then whispered to himself, "We'll see about that. . . ."

CHAPTER THIRTEEN

The school day was finally over and the students poured out of the building into the pick-up area. Tim needed to go with Tabitha. He wanted to help her. But how?

When Tabitha got into the car, Tim popped up at Tabitha's window. "Hi, Tabitha!"

Baby Tina tried to wave him away. Certainly, Carol would recognize her own husband, even if he looked like a kid. From the back seat, she tried to close the window on him, but Tim kept talking.

He introduced himself as Marcos Lightspeed, then gave his sob story. He laid it on thick, knowing Carol had a soft heart. "Well, I'd better get going if I'm gonna walk those three-and-a-half miles home. In the snow." Tim slumped over. "Without a jacket." He shivered in the cold air as he started walking away.

"Three-and-a-half miles?" Carol asked.

BYOB

CEO OF
THE YEAR

BOSS
BABY

THE ART OF
MICRO
MANAGING

NOT SO
LARGE
BUT STILL
IN CHARGE

BabyWeek

MEET
TINA
TEMPLETON

Look who's
following in
Uncle Ted's
footsteps!

Who
Wants
Cookies?
I DO!

YS

Young Suits

The magazine for the baby who has EVERYTHING

Smart Baby Gets Smarter

BOSS BABY

HE THOUGHT HE WAS OUT

But his niece pulled him back into Baby Corp.

The ABCs of
Business

Can
you get
too much
sleep?
NO
How t
POWERNA
Anytime,
anywhere
NAPtime
The magazine for the napping enthusiast

Pacifier

Soothing Grown-Ups for 25 Years

LOOK WHO'S CLOSING!

PLUS

Can Tina charm the other babies like she has her Uncle Ted?

FORMULA

FOR SUCCESS

MONEY CAN'T BUY LOVE...
OR
CAN IT?

BROTHER VS. BROTHER

Can siblings work together and still stay friends?

NINJAS
AND THE MOMS WHO LOVE THEM

PERSONS

The new
baby on the
block
TINA

"Three-and-a-half or six. Somewhere in there. Yeah, well, that TV dinner's not going to microwave itself!" Tim was overacting, and Tina rolled her eyes at him. But it worked, Carol invited Tim for dinner. He smiled as he buckled in for the ride. Tabitha was going to do well in the pageant. He'd see to that!

Boss Baby stayed behind at school. He followed the exclusive purple path until it dead-ended at the base of the tree that was in the center of the atrium. His acorn changed from yellow to purple, and then a doorway opened. Boss Baby stepped forward and fell down a giant slide! There were dips and curls and finally, with a mighty plunk, he landed in a secret underground lair.

There was a long, wide hallway lined with enormous concrete rooms. Boss Baby peeked through one of the massive windows into an observation chamber below. He saw babies with clipboards taking notes as various images flashed around them.

Boss Baby was mad at Tim for not being there with the spy camera. He took out his phone and got in position to take a photo, when a menacing shadow loomed over him. Boss Baby turned, only to find a baby ninja lurking at the end of the hallway. More baby ninjas chased him around a corner, throwing their weapons as they went.

The next hallway was a dead end! Boss Baby covered his head and expected the worst, but before the ninjas could reach him, a futuristic golf cart zoomed by and scooped him up. Boss Baby hung on for his life.

Boss Baby was surprised to discover that his hero was Dr. Armstrong.

"I see that you've angered my baby ninjas," Dr. Armstrong said casually as he shooed them away. The golf cart passed large screens displaying different apps.

"I know tuition's pretty steep, but how do you afford all this?" Boss Baby asked.

"Oh, that's a good question. I taught babies to code," Dr. Armstrong said as if it was no big deal.

The babies made the apps, and Dr. Armstrong sold them. He listed his successes: "Cat Chat, PalmDoodle. Find My Nose. StockCrush."

"I love StockCrush." Boss Baby was impressed. He asked, "So why bother with a school? You could go public and make millions."

"Billions," Dr. Armstrong corrected. "Yeah, but some things are more important than money."

"Please don't say love." Boss Baby gagged.

"Power," the doctor replied.

Boss Baby smiled. "That's more like it."

CHAPTER FOURTEEN

Carol led the kids into the house. Baby Tina kept her eyes pinned to Tim. She waited for a chance to talk to him. Finally, Carol called Tabitha in to help with dinner, leaving Tina with Tim.

"Psst, psst. Daddy!" Tina called him over to the playpen. "Where's Uncle Ted?"

"He kicked me off the mission," Tim explained.

Tina was furious. "He can't do that! Only I can do that! You're back on the mission!"

"I have my own mission now!" Tim told her.

"What could be more important than my mission?" Tina asked.

"Gotta go. Lightspeed out," Tim said, refusing to answer. He went looking for Tabitha.

"Ugh, now I have a headache!" Tina moaned, rubbing her temples.

Tim noticed a photo of himself and Ted when they were kids, and quietly turned it over. The last thing he needed was someone noticing a resemblance. Then he helped Tabitha set the table while Carol checked on dinner in the kitchen.

They talked about school, about Nathan, and then Tim asked, "So why is the pageant stressing you out so much?"

"Ugh, I have to sing," she admitted. "My whole family's going to be there, including my Dad. It's like a punch in the stomach." She tipped forward as if actually feeling the punch.

He had to ask, "You're embarrassed of him?"

"No! No, it's not that," she said.

Tim sighed loudly. He was relieved.

"It's just he's really good at this kind of thing, being creative, using your imagination. But it's hard for me. I just want him to be proud of me. You know?" she asked.

"Really?" Tim wanted to tell her that was already a fact. But he couldn't reveal himself. There was more he wanted to say, when to Tim's surprise, his parents walked in.

"Hey, hey! The key still works!" Tim's father said, slipping out of his coat.

"You guys should really change the locks," Tim's mother said. She handed Carol a stack of holiday gifts.

Tim and baby Tina shared a look of panic as Tabitha rushed to greet them.

Tina hissed to Tim, "Daddy, they're going to recognize you!"

"No, no, it's fine! I've got the glasses. See!" He raised them, then lowered them, as if the glasses changed his whole face.

Tabitha, Tim's parents, and Carol huddled together for a photo. "Selfie!" they said at the same time. They needed Tina for the photo.

"Hide!" Tina told Tim.

"Just be cool!" Tim assured her. It would be okay. The glasses were a great disguise!

"Hello! Hey, who's the new guy?" Tim's dad caught Tim through his phone camera.

"That's Marcos!" Tabitha introduced her friend.

Tim's dad took a photo of Tim. "I gotcha!"

CHAPTER FIFTEEN

Boss Baby and Dr. Armstrong entered the coding arena. Babies in hoodies and earbuds were typing away at computers surrounding a central stage. The giant screens filled with images of Armstrong's accomplishments. He gave a speech about how once he recognized he was smarter than his parents, he ran away. The most important word to a kid, he realized, was "No!"

"NO!" the baby crowd chanted in unison.

Boss Baby witnessed the massive power the doctor had over the babies.

"Take a nap!" the doctor demanded in a parent's voice.

"Nyet!" the Russian babies replied, using the Russian word for no.

Dr. Armstrong was proud. The babies were rebelling against things a parent might say, just as he'd taught them.

"Put on your coat!" he told the German kids.

"Nein!" they answered, saying no in German.

"Eat your vegetables!"

"Nahi!" the Indian babies cried out.

Dr. Armstrong gave a satisfied smile. His parents had used him as part of a study, exposing him to hours of language lessons, classical music, and public radio, which led to him becoming advanced well beyond his years. He was happy to share this knowledge with his students.

"Are you going to let grown-ups push you around?" Dr. Armstrong asked.

"No, no, no!" the babies chanted.

Dr. Armstrong turned to Boss Baby. "Are you?"

"Good God, no!" Boss Baby shouted, imitating the others.

"Why do parents get to be in charge anyway? They had their chance and what did we get? Pollution, politics, wars—" The mega-screens flashed images of worldwide destruction, ending with the atomic bomb explosion. "The only thing holding us back, is them! But not anymore! The moment we've worked so hard for is almost here.

B-Day!" Dr. Armstrong had the crowd in his hands. All the babies began cheering and clapping.

Boss Baby asked Dr. Armstrong, "B-Day?"

"It's the beginning of the baby revolution! Yay! And there will be cake! Cake for everybody!" Dr. Armstrong announced.

The babies cheered, and Boss Baby began to worry.

"No more rules! No more parents!" Dr. Armstrong said excitedly.

"Uh-oh . . ." Boss Baby's eyes widened. "This is bad."

Dr. Armstrong handed Boss Baby a root-beer float to toast his success.

Boss Baby took the drink and raised it. In a weak voice he said, "To no more parents!"

"Cheers to the revolution!" Dr. Armstrong raised his own float and the two of them clinked glasses.

Tim sat at the dinner table with his family. Tina kept looking between Tim and Tim's very own mother, who was staring.

Tim's father was scrolling past photos of young Tim, looking exactly like he did now. He reached the newer photos of Tabitha and Tina and explained that the app he used was called QTSnap. "It's so easy to share pictures on it, everyone has it!" Tim's dad told them.

"So, Marcos Lightspeed, is that what you said?" Tim's mom said the name as if it was suspicious. "It's like I know you from somewhere."

"Uh, I don't think so." Tim pushed up his glasses, securing his disguise.

"He looks just like Tim," his own father said.

Everyone turned to examine Tim, who began to sweat.

"Except Tim didn't wear glasses," Tim's dad said.

The family all nodded. It was a good point.

"Oh, that's right," Tim's mother said, lowering her glare.

Tim tipped his glasses to Tina. "Well, how about that," he brag-whispered.

"Hey, where is Tim anyway?" his father asked Carol.

"Tim and Ted are on a trip," she told them, as if that was normal.

It wasn't normal. Tim's mom gasped in shock, and asked, "Together?"

Carol said, "I just hope Tim's back in time for the pageant."

"Uh, why wouldn't he be there?" Tim asked. He was surprised when they all started to laugh.

"Tim Time," his dad said.

Carol explained, "Tabitha's father has a very active imagination. Which is a good thing." Except when it made him late or miss important things.

"Remember when he said our boss was trying to kidnap us?" Tim's mom chuckled.

Tim's dad laughed. "Or that his baby brother could walk and talk, but only when we weren't looking?!"

Those things were true! And just now, Tim was not using his imagination when he noticed Boss Baby riding Precious past the window. Or when he saw Boss Baby enter through the dog door and sneak into the house.

"You know, Ted was quite a handful, himself." Tim's mom started.

"Remember the time he sued us?" Tim's dad rolled his eyes at the memory.

"Teenagers." His mom gave a surrendered look like, *What are you going to do?"*

"He really looked up to his big brother, though," Tim's father said, which made Tim's jaw drop.

"Oh yeah. He wouldn't leave him alone," Tim's mom shared.

"Everything Tim did, Teddy wanted to do," Tim's dad said. "Tag-Along Teddy we called him.

His mother added, "Well, not to his face."

Tim didn't know any of this.

"No. No, not to his face. He was very litigious," Tim's dad said, very seriously.

"But you know what, your dad didn't mind. He was so proud of his little brother." Tim's mom smiled at the memory.

Boss Baby peeked around a corner. He had heard all of this.

"Those guys did everything together," their father said.

"They were best friends," their mom revealed.

Tabitha turned to her sister. "Just like you and me, right Tina?" She leaned over to tickle Tina, who giggled hard. "Best friends forever! Tickle monster!" Tabitha kept at it and Tina kept laughing.

"That's so sweet," Carol said, watching her girls with love.

Tim and Boss Baby were both there too. Only no one knew it.

After dinner, Tabitha showed Marcus/Tim her room. She hooked up alligator clips to the fishbowl, then attached that to a child's spelling game. "I made this vocalizer for Dr. Hawking!"

Tim recognized the toy. "Hey, my old whadidjyou-d-o-?!" He inspected the game. The back was a mess of wires and circuit boards.

"Check this out! Say hello, Dr. Hawking."

The fish spoke through the vocalizer. "HEEEEEE."

Tabitha turned away. "Um. He has performance anxiety." She began showing off other things in her room with a laser pointer. "Oh! This is Lam-Lam."

Tim smiled. "Hey, Lam-lam."

She showed him her science awards, rocks, and telescope.

Tim noticed his own guitar in the corner. "Hey, cool guitar."

"Yeah, that's my dad's," she told him.

"Hey, if you want, I can help you with your song." He took the guitar and placed his fingers, ready to strum. Tabitha refused.

"Listen, all you gotta do is imagine that you're inside the song. Everything in the lyrics is actually happening to you, and you can see the notes." As he began to strum, the molecule structure above Tabitha's bed shifted and transformed into music notes.

Maybe his imagination could save the day?

CHAPTER SIXTEEN

Tim led Tabitha on a musical adventure. The music pumped as the two of them ran down a magical hallway, with endless mystery doors.

"Marcos, wait up!" Tabitha wasn't sure how this whole imagination thing worked.

"Come on, let's go!" Tim jumped on some floating musical notes.

"A little too high!" Tabitha couldn't reach the notes. She didn't know which way to go.

"You can sing anything you want," Tim said. He encouraged her to try a few times. The notes continued to float by them, some faster than others. Tabitha decided to go for it. She belted out a song, as Tim encouraged her. When the song ended, Tabitha felt like she could conquer singing, and Tim felt like he was a really good dad.

They slowly came out of the imagination world and back into Tabitha's room.

"Thanks, Marcos!" Tabitha said with all her heart. She smiled, then realized her family was in the doorway. They'd been listening. "What—?" Ugh.

Tim's dad raised his camera. The camera flashed, then the family hurried away.

Tabitha laughed. "Oh no." That was embarrassing.

Tim was sympathetic. He shrugged and laughed, "Parents, right?"

Up in the attic, Boss Baby was working at Tim's old desk, while Tina made a call on the toy phone. No one was answering.

"Don't they understand it's the fate of the world?!" Boss Baby said. They could both hear the hold music through the phone speaker.

A voice said, *"All operators are currently napping."*

"Back in my day, we wrote memos," Boss Baby told her.

"Aw, that's cute and old timey." Tina mocked him.

Boss Baby pretended he didn't hear that, but said, "Hrmph. I weep for the future."

Baby Tina was still poking fun. She said, "So do you want to talk about your feelings now? While I'm on hold? I can give you twenty minutes."

"No." Boss Baby buried his head in paperwork.

Tina hopped on the toy train circling the attic and rode over to him. "Let's get to the nut, the nugget. What are you afraid of?"

Boss Baby was annoyed by the question. "Sharks, getting shot in the head with an arrow, and the IRS. That's it."

Baby Tina felt like they were making progress. "Finally! There you go. Was that so hard? Baby steps! Now, what about being lonely?"

"I'm not lonely! I'm just alone. There's a difference."

Tina passed him a stack of papers. "I think it's time you read your file."

He took the file and opened it. There was a single piece of paper inside.

It was a letter from Tim, written when they were young. Boss Baby gave a small gasp as he began to read.

Dear Boss Baby, I promise you this: every morning when you wake up, I will be there. Every night at dinner, I will be there. Every birthday party, every Christmas morning—I will be there. Year after year after year. And you and I will always be brothers. Always.

Boss Baby closed the file. "We were just kids. We didn't know anything about the real world. And eventually, you have to grow up." Boss Baby coughed loudly. His throat was suddenly very tight.

"Just because you grow up, doesn't mean you have to grow apart," Tina replied.

"Maybe it's already too late," Boss Baby said. Just then, Tim pulled himself over the open window frame and tumbled into the attic.

"Hey, sorry I'm late," Tim said, looking around. The room was suspiciously quiet. "What's going on?"

"Uncle Ted really misses you. Isn't that nice," Tina said, flashing a look over at Ted, who was hard at work on a project.

"So . . . whatcha doing?" Tim asked his brother.

Boss Baby revealed that he'd done surgery on Wizzie, putting He-Man's buff and bulky arm in place of his missing one.

"Look, I'm sorry about what I said at recess," Boss Baby said.

Tim accepted the apology, then said, "I was just worried about Tabitha, you know?"

Boss Baby nodded. "She's your daughter, I get it."

"This whole time I was thinking about what I wanted and not what she needed! I think I've finally got this parenting thing figured out!" Tim told them about the song practice.

"Yeah, well about that." Boss Baby had news to share. "Armstrong wants to get rid of parents. He's planning a baby revolution."

Tim couldn't believe it. "We've got to stop him!"

Boss Baby told him they were off the case. Baby

Corp. was taking over. Ted was leaving and going back to his office.

Tina watched her dad and uncle. They were not coming together. She looked at the toy phone, which was still playing hold music. An idea formed.

"Hello?" She pretended someone had answered. "So, you're not going to do anything? Well then we'll take care of it! You know what, Baby Corp.? I QUIT!" Tina hung up so dramatically, she got tangled in the phone cord. "What a bunch of diaper sniffers! Looks like we have to stop Armstrong ourselves. If you two can put up with each other a little longer."

"I suppose I can live with that. Tim?" Boss Baby asked his brother.

"I think that's doable," Tim said, a small smile formed.

"It's eight forty-five p.m.," Wizzie announced, moving his new arms around.

Time to save the world.

CHAPTER SEVENTEEN

The formula wasn't going to keep them young much longer. Boss Baby and Tim needed to get back into the school and stop Dr. Armstrong right away. That meant they had to do it at the pageant.

The idea was that Tina would be able to watch Tim and Boss Baby from her tablet. They'd have two earpieces to communicate. She called the earpieces a GAGA device. They'd translate her own baby talk into regular words. No one would be suspicious.

Tim would be onstage, in costume with the other kids, making sure everything went smoothly.

Boss Baby would stay with Dr. Armstrong. He'd attach a tiny electronic device to the principal's suit that would let Tina control the doctor's movements. When Dr. Armstrong was on stage, she'd force him to take off the suit and reveal himself as a baby.

The parents would take photos and share them. Dr. Armstrong's plans would be ruined.

And after it was over, Tina, Tim, and Boss Baby would have a pizza party.

That was the plan. This is what actually happened:

Cars filled the parking lot around the school. Parents filed into a large theater to see the pageant.

Dr. Armstrong took the stage. "Welcome, parents, to our holiday show! Remember: flash photography in the auditorium is absolutely okay! Take a picture, show your kids that you love them! Yippee!"

Like at a rock concert, lights swept the crowd.

Carol looked around for Tim. He wasn't there. His seat stayed empty.

Tim's parents held up their phones, ready to capture the pageant. A few other parents held up their phones as well. Tina put on a winter hat to cover her headphones. She checked that the coast was clear, then babbled into the GAGA device.

"Uncle Teddy, are you in position?"

Boss Baby was sitting next to Dr. Armstrong in a fancy box seat, high above the stage.

"The baby's in the cradle," Boss Baby said softly.

Tina babbled for Tim. "Papa Bear, can you read me?"

Backstage Tim was ready to go onstage in a snowflake costume. He glanced around at the activity around him. "The flake has landed."

From his box seat, Dr. Armstrong cheered the loudest. "It's starting!" He didn't mean the pageant. He meant B-Day. Dr. Armstrong explained to Boss Baby that the QTSnap app the parents were using to take photos was going to bring the revolution. Parents would soon be unnecessary as the babies took over.

"Forever starts today." Dr. Armstrong grinned widely. He logged in to his tablet and uploaded a patch.

This was very, very bad.

The curtains opened to reveal an elaborate winter wonderland. Real snow machines blew soft flakes like a blanket, as little kids and babies in snow-flake costumes ice-skated.

The song was about the dangers of global warming. *"It's Christmastime. It's the best time of the year."*

Tim was in the snowflake chorus, dancing awk-wardly as he faked the words.

Suddenly, the wintery set transformed into a pol-luted horror show. A giant snowman began to melt in the sweltering heat.

The pageant kids continued to sing. *"But due to ice caps melting, global warming is here. It feels like summer. The snow has disappeared. It's all our parents' fault, so we're all DOOMED."*

The children flopped to the ground. Tim was a beat late in recognizing what they were doing.

"Did the kids just say we're doomed?" Tim's dad stared at the kids slowly falling onstage.

Behind them, Jimbo took a photo of the kids and immediately got hypnotized. More parents began to snap pictures, and as each of their cameras flashed, their eyes went vacant.

Boss Baby could see what was happening. "Their brains are turning to mush."

"Months of hypnotic research embedded into the most user-friendly photo app ever made," Dr. Armstrong bragged. More parents took pictures with the app. The flashes went off in every corner of the auditorium. "Now all we need to do is sit back, relax, and enjoy the show."

Boss Baby told Dr. Armstrong, "Right. I'll be right back. We're outta Dundlefloofers." He updated Tina over the GAGA device as he raced to the stage. "Tina! Come in! B-Day is happening now!"

Baby Tina shouted, "What?!" over the applauding parents.

"It's all in the phones!" Boss Baby told her. There was only one thing to do. "We have to stop the show."

CHAPTER EIGHTEEN

Baby Tina pulled up a map of the theater on her tablet. She tried to reach Tim, but his earpiece was on the ground. He was watching Tabitha get ready to sing. He walked right past the main electrical breaker, which would have shut everything down, but he didn't hear Tina asking him to turn off the power.

Boss Baby ran to the backstage entrance but was blocked by two baby theater techs dressed in black jumpsuits. He noticed a line of babies in nativity costumes about to go onstage.

Tabitha was about to perform. Meghan, dressed as a present, told her, "Don't mess up!"

From the theater wings, Tim watched Tabitha step out onstage. He quickly discovered that Boss Baby was already out there, hiding in the manger.

Boss Baby leaped up and began tap-dancing toward Tim singing, *"We have to shut down the pageant! Armstrong is using an app to brainwash the parents!"* He came offstage and went to pull the lever on the main power breaker, but Tim stopped him.

"You'd risk the future of the world to see your daughter sing?" Boss Baby asked.

"Yes!" Tim looked over at Tabitha, who was now on top of the tree getting ready for her solo.

"You're crazy!" Boss Baby struggled to reach the lever.

The brothers began to fight, rolling around and wrestling until Dr. Armstrong broke them up. He knew they'd been working together. When Boss Baby asked how he knew, Dr. Armstrong told him, "The bickering, the petty disputes, the jealousy— you know you two could only be brothers. You're opposites in every way and yet completely codependent."

The power switch turned out to be a trap. Just as Tabitha began her song, Baby Ninjas came to take Boss Baby and Tim to the time-out room. Tim tried to break free, he wanted to hear Tabitha sing! But they were forced down into the Box and strapped to chairs. Mellow music played, and a fountain gurgled softly. Then, the water in the fountain began to overflow, splashing across the floor and rising quickly.

Tim began to panic as the water reached the chairs.

"This isn't a time out. It's game over," Tim said sadly.

In the auditorium, the children finished their song. Everyone turned to face Tabitha.

She was standing over the theater at the top of a massive Christmas tree. Tabitha took a deep breath, and began to sing a holiday song about the importance of family.

"Catch my eye. Take my hand. This bond is tighter than we ever planned. Give me courage so I can land. We know that divided we'll all fall, so together we stand."

Tabitha's performance was so moving that every

single audience member who wasn't already hypnotized was capturing it on their phones, including
Carol and Tim's Mom.

She finished, letting the final note hang in the air.
It was so emotional, no one dared make a sound in
the entire auditorium. Even Nathan was impressed.

Blinded by the stage lights, Tabitha couldn't
see the audience. One person began to clap. She
squinted, hoping it was her dad, but it was Tina.
She could see now that Tim's seat was empty.

From the audience, Tina saw Tabitha's smile fade.
"Oh, Tabitha . . ." Tina began, then she noticed her
hypnotized family. And every other hypnotized adult
in the room. "Oh no!" Tina snuck out of her seat.
She desperately whispered into the GAGA, "Dad,
Uncle Ted! Come in, come in, where are you?"

Thinking everyone was staring because they
hated the song, Tabitha burst into tears and ran off
the stage.

Dr. Armstrong went on the stage and ordered the

hypnotized parents to give her a standing ovation. They stood like zombies and clapped.

Dr. Armstrong turned to the babies. "We did it! The baby revolution has begun!"

Behind him, the Christmas tree opened to reveal a giant cake.

"No more need for costumes!" Dr. Armstrong sprung out of his grown-up suit, revealing a baby-size version of his tuxedo. "Happy B-Day, everybody!"

"Oh my gosh!" Meghan said seeing him as a baby.

Nathan fainted.

"All right, come on, cake for everybody!" Dr. Armstrong stepped aside as the babies hungrily rushed for the cake.

CHAPTER NINETEEN

Alone on the steps, Tabitha sniffled. Baby Tina handed her a tissue. "Here you go, Sis. Come on, don't cry."

Tabitha looked up. "Wait. Are you talking?"

"A little bit!" Tina shrugged.

"Ahhhh! Oh my gosh, you're talking!" Tabitha was shocked.

"I have to, it's an emergency! I'm on a super-secret mission from Baby Corp.!" Tina told her.

"You mean Dad's stories are true?" Tabitha couldn't believe it.

Tina explained the mission and that they had to go find Ted and Tim. She said, "Dr. Armstrong is a baby. A very bad, bad baby." Tina needed her sister's help.

Tabitha knew that to disable the app, they needed to reach the computer server that was in the acorn at the top of the atrium tree.

The girls were about to run off to the atrium when

Tina noticed the control chip they'd intended to use in Dr. Armstrong's suit was on the floor. She told Tabitha that they needed to go to Dr. Armstrong's dressing room first.

The water in the time-out chamber was almost at the ceiling. Tim and Boss Baby had floated up and were gasping for air.

"It looks like this is it, Tim," Boss Baby said, taking a huge gulp of oxygen. He took the last few minutes to tell Tim that he was a great dad.

Tim admitted that he'd always been jealous of Boss Baby's success.

"Well, hey, at least we have these final precious moments together," Tim said, filling his own lungs for one last time.

"Precious!" Wait, that was it! Boss Baby whistled for the pony.

Outside, Precious's ears perked up. She sprinted toward the sound and burst into the school. Precious knocked down the time-out room door. Water flowed out. Tim and Boss Baby rode the waves into the hallway. They were free!

"That's my girl!" Boss Baby hugged the pony.

Tim went to thank Precious too, but the horse spit water in his face. Coughing hard and wiping at his face, Tim grabbed his GAGA device. "Tina, come in! It's Daddy!"

Tabitha and Tina were in Dr. Armstrong's dressing room. They were looking at one of his adult-size leisure suits.

"Dad! Listen, we have to shut down the server. It's in the acorn!" Tina told Tim over the GAGA.

"Whoa! This is so weird." Tabitha had lived with Tina her whole life and never heard her talk. She'd also lived with Tim her whole life and never believed his stories.

Tim and Boss Baby were headed to the atrium tree. All of a sudden, baby ninjas sprung out of their hiding spots. They were about to attack, but when they began to move, they discovered they were standing in a river of glue.

"Glueee!" Glue Baby came into view.

Bo Peep burst into the hallway throwing confetti at the ninjas. "Pixie dust!"

The babies from the yellow room had all come to help. Creepy Girl was at the end of the hall. The lights began to flicker. She snuck closer and closer to one of the ninjas, who didn't notice her there.

"I like your pajamas!" she cooed at him. The ninja ran away from her.

"I'm proud to be a yellow!" Boss Baby saluted his classmates as Precious carried him and Tim around a corner.

In the doctor's dressing room, Tabitha and Tina each climbed into one of his suits.

"Now let's crack that big nut," Tina said, pointing the way to the atrium tree, the big acorn tree house, and the only way to stop this madness.

Dr. Armstrong was talking to his baby programmers. He was back in his robotic suit. He saw Tim and Ted and announced, "Nothing's gonna ruin my B-Day. Not even you."

The screens behind him switched images to reveal a massive B-Day countdown clock.

Boss Baby and Tim exchanged a look as they ran toward them.

"Glue me." Boss Baby put out his hands and Tim loaded them with glue. Then Boss Baby did the same for Tim. They scrambled up the tree toward the server as fast as they could.

Precious tried to stop the doctor herself, but he managed to toss her out of the room. Then, the doctor took two huge sticky lollipops and used them to yank Tim and Boss Baby off the tree by the seat of their pants. He said that Boss Baby could have been his partner.

Boss Baby looked warmly at his brother. "I've already got a partner."

There was a *CRASH* at the back of the room. Everyone turned to see Tina arrive. She was wearing one of Dr. Armstrong's leisure suits. Tabitha was riding on her back. Tina was able to control the suit with the device implanted in the back.

Tabitha looked from Tim to Tina and back to Tim again. Suddenly it all clicked.

"So, Marcos is really Dad?" Tabitha said.

"Yep!" Tina answered.

Tabitha let out a long sigh. "I said a lot to that kid."

Things were not looking good for Dr. Armstrong. So he removed a large button from his suit and pressed it. He called the hypnotized parents from the theater to the atrium. "Hug them to death!" he commanded.

The parents surged forward toward Tim and Boss Baby shouting, "Hugs! Hugs!"

Tim told Tina that he and Boss Baby would deal with the zombie parents. She needed to take Tabitha to the server.

Dr. Armstrong's suit had power and he used it to leap up the tree, following the girls.

The girls were in trouble. The zombie parents were trying to hug the boys to death. Could this be the end?

CHAPTER TWENTY

Tabitha and Tina continued toward the server room at the top of the tree in the atrium. There was a hand scanner to enter the room. Tina used the suit's control device to get Dr. Armstrong to open it. They burst into a large computer server room with white floors, white ceiling, and white paneled computers lining the walls. Dr. Armstrong chased Tabitha, but Tina tripped him. She was doing everything she could to give Tabitha time.

Tabitha guessed the password and began to search for a way to shut it all down.

Below the tree and the server room, in the wide school atrium, the parent and grandparent zombies continued to try to hug Tim and Boss Baby to death.

"Give me a hug," their father moaned.

"I'll sue you! You know I will!" Boss Baby threatened.

Up in the acorn server room, Tina and Dr. Armstrong duked it out. Candy flew out of his suit.

Tabitha managed to find the shutdown command. But just before she hit the key to terminate the whole program, Dr. Armstrong slammed his fist through the computer terminal.

"B-Day will happen whether you like it or not!" Dr. Armstrong announced.

Tabitha's eyes darted from Armstrong to the sprinkler system above. She ran over to the entrance of the acorn and shouted down the tree. "Dad! Uncle Ted! Pull the fire alarm!"

Tim and Boss Baby were engulfed in the zombie horde.

"No, no, no, stop! Stop, stop, stop!" Tim tried to end the madness.

"God no! No kissies! No kissies!" Boss Baby was horrified by his loving parents.

Wizzie burst from Tim's backpack. "Time's up,

halflings!" The formula was running out of power and the boys would start to grow.

The swarm of parents closed around Tim and Boss Baby. Suddenly, a teenaged Boss Baby burst from the center of the parents, tossing Tim aside to safety. "Tim, get to the fire alarm! Make it rain, baby!"

Tim found the alarm. He pulled the lever. A single drip of water plopped out of the sprinklers.

Dr. Armstrong laughed. "The school's expensive. I had to cut costs someplace, you know." The doomsday timer continued to tick toward zero.

The countdown struck zero.

They were too late. Dr. Armstrong poured himself a celebratory cup of soda.

Tabitha noticed that the candy Dr. Armstrong had been carrying in his pocket, which now scattered on the floor, was Mentos. The soda was in his hand. She remembered the science project! Mentos and soda together would fizz into a volcano! Tabitha scooped a handful of candies off the floor and gave them to Tina.

"Here's to B-Day." Dr. Armstrong raised his cup.

"Of doom!" Tina and Tabitha shouted at the same time. They charged forward dropping Mentos into Dr. Armstrong's cup.

"What the—?" Dr. Armstrong exclaimed as his drink began to foam. The liquid spilled over the edge of the cup and onto the server, which began to spark. "No!"

Tina and Tabitha flung soda and Mentos all over the server room. The foam exploded and filled the room.

Dr. Armstrong screamed as the server blew up. Tina jammed her control device into the back of his suit and hit an eject button on her tablet. Dr. Armstrong was hurtling toward the ground when Tina trapped him by his underwear, giving the doctor a super-wedgie.

Tabitha fell off the tree, when Tim suddenly grew back to adult size and caught her. She gave him a kiss on the cheek, which made him smile wider than he'd ever smiled before.

"I love you, Tabitha Templeton," Tim told his daughter.

Tina raised her hands and prepared to jump out of the tree. "Uncle Ted, heads up!"

Ted caught her.

Tina laughed. "Get ready to order some pizzas!"

All around the world, Acorn Centers powered down.

The parents began returning to normal. Throughout the atrium, there were joyful reunions as kids found their parents and gave real, not deadly, hugs.

Bo Peep found her mom. Glue Baby jumped into Jimbo's arms. Creepy Girl cuddled up to Precious.

Ted turned to Tim and Tina. "Not bad, Templetons."

"Yeah, mission accomplished!" Tim said.

"And as a bonus we stopped Armstrong, too!" Tina said. Ted and Tim looked confused. Wasn't that the whole reason they were there? To stop Dr. Armstrong? Tina explained, "My real mission was to get you guys back together again. That wasn't obvious?"

"So, you never actually quit?" Ted asked.

"Nope." Baby Tina gave him a huge wink.

"Well played, Templeton." Ted was impressed.

"I don't like to mix the two, but I will say it was never business; it was always personal," Tina told them.

"You know what kid?" Ted gave her a heartfelt smile. "You're the best boss I ever had."

Tim's parents and Carol found the family. They were all so happy to see Tim had made it to the pageant after all. Ted and Tim's dad pulled out his phone to take a picture.

"Oh, come on. Everybody get together—"

Tim tried to stop him. "Dad, no!"

He was too late. The camera flashed.

EPILOGUE

It was Christmas morning at the Templeton house. Tabitha was singing her song, re-creating the performance that her dad missed. The whole family was there. Even Precious was lying on her new fluffy pony bed. The only one missing was Uncle Ted.

"We know that divided we'll fall, so together we stand," Tabitha sang.

Tim played along on his guitar, and when the song finished, Tabitha took a long, deep bow. "Thank you, thank you!"

She rushed over to give her dad a big hug. They all wished Uncle Ted had been there.

Just then, the doorbell rang.

Tim rushed forward, hopeful that it was Ted, but when he opened the door, no one was there. But, there was a note.

Tim read it out loud:

Merry Christmas, Tim. I'm sorry I couldn't be there
with you, but please enjoy this inappropriately lavish
gift instead.

Tim looked up and found a massive gold statue
of himself on the driveway. Gilded Tim was holding
a World's Greatest Dad mug.

The note went on:

You've given me the greatest gift of all—you.

Love, the best brother in the world

Tim shook his head, chuckling to himself. Then
he saw a little note on the bottom of the page.

P.S. Duck.

Huh? A snowball hit him right between the eyes.

"In your face, Leslie!" Ted shouted, teasing Tim as if they were kids.

"Hey! It is on, Lindsey!" Tim wiped the snow off his face and gave chase, scooping up snow as he ran.

Tim and Ted's dad watched his boys. "It's so great to see them fighting again."

Tabitha and Tina grabbed their coats. They were going to join the fun, when suddenly, Tina's toy phone rang.

Tabitha stopped. "Shouldn't you pick up?"

"Nah, we got some family business," Tina said softly, so no one could hear except Tabitha. They both hurried outside. Their grandparents were right behind them.

Carol picked up the receiver.

A voice said, "We have another assignment for you."

Carol stared at the phone, then looked outside at her family playing in the snow. She put on her best baby voice and said, "I'm listening."

Across town, Dr. Armstrong approached the one house with lights still on. He knocked on the door.

The people who opened the door were his parents. They welcomed him inside with a big hug. The Armstrong family was back together. This time, the doctor would do things right and enjoy each and every moment.

The End